I0530575

Trey's Room

Marty Herzog

This is for Trey
and anyone still getting through the dark.

1

"I will never forget this day!" I remember joyfully calling out as I threw my baseball mitt up in the air, watched it go higher than the power line, and caught it when it came back down. Not sure why I had my mitt with me that day, I didn't particularly like playing little league baseball and did so only because my parents wanted me to. My friend Danny and I were playing in the empty field next to my house. He lived in an apartment complex across the street and down about a half a block. Sometimes while visiting him over there, I joined in on spontaneous dodge ball games that were played against the concrete brick barrier that separated the courtyard from the street.

I don't know why this day stood out so much to me, but it did. Perhaps it was because nothing else interfered with the pure joy of just being and playing, that I had forgotten about everything else. But I think there's also another reason, this day was supposed to be remembered. Earlier Danny and I had ridden our bikes around the neighborhood and stopped by the convenience store a few blocks away to buy candy. When we came back, we acted out a movie I had made up, something I did often by myself but it was fun to also have someone else join in.

This takes place in the 1970's, stating that now because I'll be doing some things that might raise an eyebrow if done today. Can't say it was a simpler time for me, but a kid could do a lot more things in a seemingly safe way. It certainly wasn't a more innocent time—the threats that permeate our day-to-day existence just hadn't made their presence fully known yet.

You won't believe me about this, am stating that now also. A good deal of it, sure, but not all of it. It's a difficult thing to realize that my life is something no one will ever fully understand.

I am writing this to help me figure out why things have turned out the way they have, a mea culpa if you will.

What is it that you remember when you think back on your childhood?

A few years before this, my parents and I along with some extended family rented a beach house. On one of the nights they decided to tell ghost stories. An uncle had sneaked off and started shining a flashlight on the building next to us to add to the spooky atmosphere, simple but effective on fairly young me. One of the supposed true stories was there was a relative on my father's side who saw something one night that made his hair turn completely white, and it remained that way the rest of his life. He would never say what it was, but he was never quite the same person afterwards.

But back to this day. Danny's mom called over to us that it was time for him to come home. I gave him a big hug and watched him cross the street. I danced a bit and spun around so much that I fell to the grass to let the dizziness pass. I didn't want the day to end, but figured I should head home because it was probably getting close to being time for dinner. I had already parked my bike in the garage so just had to grab my mitt. I started walking in the small ditch that ran beside the street. As I walked, I remembered a particularly rainy day when I donned my raincoat and boots and walked through the water in this ditch while it was still raining. As I got closer, I could see the window of my room on which I had hung a picture that I drew for people to see as they drove by.

The house was one story, all wood and painted completely white. My room faced the street and next to mine in the corner was my sister's room. Next to that was a bathroom and then my parent's room which faced the back yard. In between was a long hallway that had an attic fan with slats that opened up when it was turned on. Next to my parent's room was my grandmother's room, next to that the kitchen, and in the center of the house was the living room. Two pine trees stood in the front yard close to the door on which my father had hung a tire swing. The garage was in the back of the house along with a large back yard enclosed by a chain link fence. On the other side of the house was another empty field, this one completely unkept with grass always growing quite high. Directly across the street were trailer homes.

I was almost to the driveway that went over the ditch when I saw it. Our cat was laying in the middle of the road and not moving. I gasped three times in succession. I stood there waiting to see if maybe he would get up, but he didn't. I ran through the front door calling out for Mom. She was in the kitchen next to the stove. I told her what I saw, she turned off the knobs and went outside. I went and sat on the couch in the living room.

We had gotten that cat when once we went to the beach and came back to our car and found him lying in the back seat. Did picked him up and put him out, but he jumped right back in again. So we ended up taking him home with us. He was completely black and Mom named him Midnight.

After sitting there awhile, I went into my room. I sat on the floor and thought about how fun it was having that cat. Both Mom and Dad came in, Mom had some donuts she must have gone and bought, but I didn't want any. Dad explained that the cat had been run over and died. Later that night when I was in bed, she gave me the nametag that was on Midnight's collar. I held it in my hand. Dad then came in and stood over my bed.

"Do animals go to heaven" I asked.

He looked down at me and didn't say anything for a moment. "No, animals don't have souls." He didn't say anything else and walked away. He was a pastor, so that was the end of that. I put Midnight's nametag on the nightstand and closed my eyes feeling awful.

2

My morning routine was always the same. Dad would wake me up, I would get dressed and join him in the kitchen for breakfast which consisted of fried eggs, sometimes there was oatmeal. When my sister got older, he branched out to pancakes and even biscuits, but she was only four years old then and spent mornings in the living room watching television. Mom would sometimes join us at the breakfast table and my grandmother didn't come in until a couple hours later. I was still feeling sad and thought about asking Dad if I could stay home from school, but thought better of it not wanting to make him mad and so cleaned my plate. As I brushed my teeth and grabbed my schoolbooks, I heard the familiar theme song, "they call him Flipper, Flipper, faster than lightning…"

I exited through the back door in the kitchen which led to a concrete patio between the house and garage, went through the side door of the garage and grabbed my bike, came back out and left through the fence gate that was also off the patio. I got on and started peddling down the gravel driveway which was always full of pine needles, sometimes I had to dodge pine cones. At the street I took a right and began my morning commute with a gentle wind blowing against my face.

There was never very much traffic and only two major thoroughfares I had to use. I guess I was a good bike rider, I never crashed and only once remember riding across the street, hearing a car honk and looking back to see an older driver shaking his finger at me as he drove by. In less than ten minutes, I arrived and parked in the student bike parking that was outlined in red next to the school building. I retrieved my schoolbooks from the front basket leaving the bike as it was and walked in towards the cafeteria.

All six grades gathered there in the morning before classes began. The lower grades were down one hallway with the administrative offices, the upper grades were down another hall that included the music room and equipment storage room. At the beginning of this 5th grade year, I was chosen to be one of two students who every Friday afternoon gathered up the overhead and film projectors that were on rolling carts and put them away in that equipment room.

The bell rang and the students headed out. Each grade was comprised of four classrooms that were all in one open air large room with no dividers. Students were placed into each classroom according to their test scores for each subject, so there were at least a few students who changed classes each period. Social order was already being established, we just didn't realize it. We students stored our books and personals in colored tubs assigned to us that were kept in cubbies that lined the outer walls of each classroom.

The first class was math and I sat next to Jackie. He wore a retainer and did this bit where he would use each of his hands to become two creatures he called Fee and Fi. His thumb and index finger would act as the mouths while the remaining three fingers stood straight up unless they needed to bend some to show some kind of emotion. They would often get into disagreements and tussle with each other. Occasionally they would lapse into talking like John Wayne and end sentences with the word 'pilgrim'. I thought it was hilarious.

Language arts was next with our teacher Ms. Barkley. She wore these great '70s striped outfits. I remember her talking one morning about seeing Elton John in concert but referring to him as Pinball Wizard. It was in her class I came to realize how much I enjoyed reading the stories she assigned. This was the year I also started wearing eyeglasses. After that was recess and then lunch. In the afternoon was social studies, science, PE and also music class which consisted of the students sitting in chairs facing the piano which was at the front of the room that the music teacher played. We sang popular songs from the radio, the lyrics hand-written on mimeographed sheets of paper. It was such a unique sensation to smell those sheets just after they were run off.

On this day at recess, I went and stood on the cement slab in the rear of the school and saw Michael sitting by himself next to some bushes in the large field where we sometimes played kickball. He was loud and had lots of red hair and freckles. He had once invited me to his birthday party at which some of us started trading Wacky Packages which were all the rage and similar to baseball cards except they were of consumer products renamed to be somewhat gross and humorous. He saw me too and waved me over then asked if I wanted to meet him at his mother's beauty shop after school. I told him I would.

On the other side of the open field where Danny and I had played were the two buildings that made up the church that Dad was pastor at. The parish hall which was where Kindergarten was held where I met Danny, and the church building itself. On the other side of those was the beauty shop. I had gone over there a couple times before. When I got there on this day, his Mom was doing hair in the front area, so Michael said for us to go back outside and around to the back. He opened the door to a storage room. The room's floor was painted all black and we went inside and sat down. He got up and turned off the lights. We sat that way in the dark for a few moments.

"Do you know what a Benji is?" he asked nonchalantly.

"A what?"

"It comes out of your closet at night. You have to watch out for them."

What was he talking about? I had never heard of one of those before.

We went back outside and played in the front parking lot until his Mom stuck her head out the door and called that it was time for them to go home.

I had already parked my bike in the garage after school, so now had to walk home. I went in-between the church building and parish hall and got a drink from the water fountain nestled in there, then meandered down the backside of the building and into the open field. The sun was starting to set.

I never liked the night and having to go to bed and thinking about all the bad things that could happen while alone and in the dark. I was afraid of someone breaking into the house. Also about a year and a half earlier, the movie "The Exorcist" opened in movie theaters. I was of course too young to see it, but it was talked about incessantly by people. One night my parents and I were on the way home from someplace and stopped at a convenience store. I got out of the car with Dad and went inside and saw pictures of the girl in all of the possession make-up on the front cover of some of the magazines lining the rack. Seeing that really frightened me and I became afraid of being possessed. And now hearing about this Benji?

We had supper and then I finished some homework. I brushed my teeth and got into my pajamas. I always kept my bedroom door open at night. I shut my eyes as tightly as possible. Oh please, please let me fall asleep before Dad does so I'm not the only one still awake. I heard the turning of the pages of the newspaper which was a good sign because that meant he was still up. I lay very still with my eyes closed.

But soon I heard the sound of the newspaper being folded up and the click of the lamp being turned off. Dad had gone to bed. The entire house was in darkness now and completely silent.

My eyes remained shut. If someone broke in, would they be able to hurt me or even take me away before my parents could get to my room? I looked out into the darkness. Everything that was so familiar during the daytime looked so strange and different at night. I wondered how long it would be until I could finally fall asleep.

I'm not sure how much time had gone by when something happened I had never experienced before. I heard someone quietly say my name, except it was in my head. It was very faint, but I could hear it in my mind all the same. "Trey," it whispered. Then I heard a muffled thud from inside the closet. I opened my eyes and looked at the ceiling. I waited. Nothing, and then again came the muted sound from inside of the closet. My body became rigid as pain began to prickle down my legs and up my sides. I felt my chest rapidly rise and fall as I tried to catch my breath. The door handle rattled and then I heard the sound of the door slowly opening.

I turned my head towards the closet. The only light was from the streetlights outside coming through the curtains. A figure slowly lumbered out. The smell of excrement filled my nostrils. It let out a grunt each time it lurched forward. I could barely make it out, but I could see two arms, two legs, a torso and head. It seemed to be covered by something like moss, or maybe a coat of fur. It made its way over to my desk. It picked up the model airplane that I had recently put together and ran its fingers over it. When it was finished, it put that back down and picked up one of my toy cars. The car fit completely in one of its hand and it held it there. It put that back then picked up my Magic 8-Ball and held it in both of its hands.

Out of my throat came a sound like I was trying to say something but didn't know how to make words. It was my voice but strangely high pitched and against sandpaper, and I didn't even realize I was trying to make it. Putting the toy back down, it looked over at me and let out a low, guttural growl.

That snapped me out of whatever trance I seemed to be in. I leapt out of bed, my feet hit the floor and I raced out of my room.

I ran down the hallway to my parent's bedroom crying out, "There's a Benji in my room, there's a Benji in my room!" Once there I screamed it again and jumped up and down. Dad got out of bed, but Mom just sat up and stayed under the covers.

"What are you saying?" he looked down at me annoyingly and walked out. I went over and pushed myself into the far corner of the room.

"A Benji's in my room," I said again.

After a while my Dad came back in. "Trey, there's nothing there."

"But I saw it come out of the closet!"

"Come with me," he answered. I didn't move. "Now."

I followed him down the hall and into my bedroom. The light was on.

"See, nothing here."

"But it was here! See it left the closet door open."

Dad didn't say anything for a moment. "I did that when I checked inside. Now you need to stop this nonsense and get back into bed."

"But..."

"Trey!" He didn't let me finish. He grabbed my arm and led me to the bed. "You were probably having a bad dream. Sometimes they can seem real. Now stop this and go to sleep."

He turned out the light and left. The house was completely quiet again. As if what just happened didn't actually happen. I grabbed my pillow and brought it with me into the living room and sat down on the couch. I don't think I ever fell back to sleep. When I heard Dad stirring in his room in the morning, I went back into my bedroom.

I told you that you wouldn't believe me.

3

I went to the closet to start getting dressed. I looked around inside, but nothing seemed out of place. The clothes were hanging there undisturbed and my games were still on the top shelf like always.

I went to the kitchen and sat down. I could immediately tell that Dad was still annoyed about what happened last night. I was groggy from not getting any sleep.

"Look alive!" he commanded as I stared at my eggs without eating. I shook my head back and forth and ate as quickly as I could so as not to make him angrier. As soon as I was finished, I left for school.

I wanted very badly to find Michael and tell him what had happened. After parking my bike, I walked into the cafeteria and looked around, but couldn't find him. Sometimes you could hear him even if you didn't see him, but not this morning. I did find Jackie and sat down next to him. I didn't feel much like talking to anyone else and thankfully Fe and Fi had a lot to say.

At recess I walked around and saw Michael playing with three girls. I went over to him and the girls started giggling and ran off.

"Michael the Benji..."

"Hold that thought," he said smiling while walking backwards and wagging his finger, then ran off chasing them. I waited there but they never came back before we had to go inside for lunch.

I tried to see what table he was eating at but couldn't find him with all the grades being there also. I wasn't that hungry but got my tray and tried. I wasn't sure what class he was in during the afternoon and still couldn't locate him.

I rode my bike home after school. Usually the first thing I did was watch "Ultraman" on television, but today went to the front yard. Hearing voices, I looked up and saw the teenagers from the youth group gathered at the front of the church building. A few of those boys took to calling me 'pastor's kid' at church functions.

It was from this vantage point that I watched a small, gray dog start to cross the street. Suddenly an old pick-up truck was right on top of it, engulfing it and running over it. The pick-up kept going, and at first the dog lay completely still. But then it screamed, barking and flinging its head back and snarling as if something was attacking it from behind. Its hind legs were flattened out and not moving. I could see a tire track on its back. Then the little dog turned its head back around and put it down. It didn't move or make another sound. I heard one of the girls in the youth group say, "Someone should put it in the dumpster."

Horrified, I went to the backyard. I could not understand the cruelty of this happening and the girl saying something like that.

I tried my best to eat dinner to not get into trouble. It became time for bed. What was I going to do? What do you do about a Benji that comes out of your closet at night? I didn't even try to fall asleep before Dad did, just stared at the closet door. When I was younger, I sometimes went and slept on the floor beside my parent's bed. But I was forbidden to do that now that I was older. Once I heard the lamp being turned off and Dad going to bed, I took my pillow and went and lied down on the couch. The next thing I knew, I opened my eyes hearing Dad in the kitchen. I quickly went to my room and got into bed so I would be there when he came to wake me up. It seemed that the Benji didn't come out last night for some reason.

During recess at school, I finally found Michael. This time there was no one with him and I went over to him.

"The Benji came out of my closet. I don't know what to do."

His eyes got big and he thought for a moment.

"It's yours now. It will feed off your fear and want to take you away for its own." He nodded solemnly at me and walked away.

4

The next morning, I awoke with a start. I tried to get my bearings and realized that last night I was planning on just waiting in bed for Dad to go to sleep and then moving to the couch, but I must have accidently fallen asleep. Again, for some reason the Benji didn't come out.

It was Saturday, and like every Saturday morning, that meant watching cartoons. I went into the living room and turned on the television but was distracted by the predicament I was in. When they were over late morning, I started the list of chores Dad always had for me, consisting of things like vacuuming the car and mowing the grass. When I finished those, it was time for the matinee that was shown on Saturday afternoons at the movie theater. Mom dropped me off like usual, and I went to the concession stand and bought candy. Today was "Godzilla vs. the Smog Monster" which I really liked but my mind wouldn't completely let go of my own situation.

Mom picked me up and stated that she needed to return a casserole dish to one of the women who was in our church. When we arrived, she met us at the door and had short brown hair with lots of laugh lines. She had a son but said that he was not home because he was visiting a friend. She showed us his room which had quite a number of trophies. There was also a light switch cover that had his name on it with a drawing of a boy in a football uniform. I had never won a trophy for anything and was not good at sports. I wasn't one of those popular boys at school and began to feel bad about that.

We got home and I started listening to some of the records I had. There was one series that had booklets with pictures and the words printed out so I could sing along. It was still light outside, so I thought I would ride my bike before it became nighttime. I drove over to the junior high and high school which were just a few blocks away. There were tennis courts in between the two buildings and next to those I saw a family with two kids also putting down a blanket for a picnic. The dad was smiling and handing out sandwiches from the basket. He ruffled the boy's hair. My father never seemed to be pleasant like that when he was with me, it was as if he disapproved of whatever I was doing. I wondered what it would be like to be in a family like the one I was watching.

I headed back towards the church. Behind the beauty shop were two small apartments that Michael had said his mother also owned. In one of those lived an older man who I would go visit when I saw that he was outside. He was today, and we talked for a while. He was always pleasant and seemed to genuinely want to know how school was going and what I was up to. It was so nice when I talked to other adults who genuinely seemed like they enjoyed talking to me.

After that I went home. Mom and Grandma were making supper and Mom told me to wash my hands and set the table. I did and walked back through the living room where Mom was playing one of her eight track tapes, this one of Charlie Rich. A lot of time she played musical soundtracks and I would lip sync and act out the words in the hallway. Dad came home grumpy from writing the sermon for tomorrow like usual. We ate and for dessert Grandma had made homemade ice cream. It was not as thick as the kind from the store and had more ice crystals, but it was still good. When we were finished, I helped clear the table.

Mom turned on the television as it was time for Lawrence Welk. One time he picked a lady out of the audience to dance with and her wig fell off. I felt really bad for her that this happened on television for everyone to see. Grandma always watched this show with us and then would go to her room. I didn't want it to already be time for bed, so I waited for a few moments and then followed her to her room.

She had come to live with us a few years earlier after living with one of my aunts. My parents had told me she had gotten sick and needed to be in a bigger city where there were better doctors, so she came to stay with us. She had cancer. When I went into her room, she had already sat down in her recliner and was reading from this little book that she read from every night. Her hair always looked like she had just come from the beauty shop.

"Grandma, can I stay here for a little while before I go to bed?"

She jumped just a bit. "Oh, I didn't hear you come in." She looked at me like she was sensing something. "What is wrong?"

I really wanted to tell her but decided not to. "I just don't want to be alone right now."

She kept looking at me. "All right you can stay." I sat down next to her and leaned against the chair and she resumed reading. In between the chair and her bed was a small bookshelf against the wall. On it were some silver and gold trinkets and a small net with feathers hanging off it.

"What is that book about?"

"Something I brought over with me to this country when I was younger. It says things in it I want to be sure and remember."

"Is it from church?"

"No. It's something else."

She had a pretty quilt over her legs that she had sewn. I stood up and touched some of the colorful blocks. I looked at her noticing her clear eyes behind the glasses. "Goodnight, Grandma."

"Goodnight, Trey."

I walked down the hall. Dad and Mom were still in the living room, my little sister had already been put to bed. I got out one of my books that I had ordered at school from the Scholastic Book Catalog. The forms were handed out every few weeks and sometimes I used my allowance to buy books and sometimes I asked Mom for extra money. I had quite a collection and made my own library using index cards I had gotten for a project at school and gave each book one. After reading it for a while, I got up and got my paper and began writing my own story about a spaceship that lands on earth. Dad stuck his head through the doorway and told me it was time to go to sleep because I needed to get up in the morning for Sunday school. He left and I put on my pajamas then walked through the living room to the doorway to Grandma's room. Her door was always shut when she was sleeping. I sat down and leaned against the wall. The next thing I knew Dad was picking me up and taking me to my room. I must have fallen asleep and he always got up very early on Sunday mornings. We got to my room and he set me down on the floor crossly.

"We are not going to get into this habit again. Understand?"

I told him that I did.

5

After church, I called my friend Laura to talk and she asked if I wanted to come over, so I asked Mom who said yes. We had first met when she rode back and forth with us to the parochial school I went to before the public school I was now in. That private school was such a safe environment for me with its small class sizes. But in 4th grade I was taken out of there and placed in a school whose ways I didn't understand. Some of the boys were mean to me which I was not used to. The big thing all the kids talked about was getting into fights. I had never been in one and had absolutely no idea what to do if I ever did get in one, so became fearful of it. Most infamous for fighting was a kid named Bruce who had dark hair that almost covered his eyes, a sullen attitude and perpetual frown. I avoided him at all costs.

Mom went to get her purse and we got into the car. She dropped me off and I walked through their open garage and knocked on the door. I was greeted by her mom, a tall, slender woman who had a wonderful laugh. I had observed her hugging Laura a couple times which was something my parents never did; they never physically touched me unless Dad was punishing me. Laura's Mom brought me to the front room where she was laying on her stomach listing to an album. We did that for a while and then started playing with her two Barbies and their accessories. I liked playing with her dolls even more than with my own GI Joe. Her Mom came in later and said I could stay for supper that night and that she had already called my mother to let her know.

We sat at their table which was next to their kitchen and looked out into the backyard. Her dad was working late that night. It was always a jovial experience eating with them and it made me feel good because there was so much affection that they showed to each other and also to me. Across from the table was their living room where Laura's Mom said she had hung a painting that she just finished which was of flowers in a vase. For dessert we had her homemade chocolate cake which my Mom had gotten the recipe for.

It was wonderful being with Laura and her mom, but it came time for me to go home and Mom came by and picked me up. It was dark by now and when we got home, I asked Dad if I could stay up and watch television, but of course he said no and that it was time for bed.

I got ready and then lay there with absolutely no idea of what to do for myself. I listened to the familiar noises coming from the living room, and then came the inevitable folding up of the newspaper and sound of the lamp being turned off. I waited with apprehension, but surprisingly ended up falling asleep and awoke realizing the Benjy didn't come out last night.

At breakfast Dad announced the baseball leagues were starting up again and that I was going to play, and this would be the year I was going to learn to not be afraid of the ball. Mom added that I needed to lose weight. The YMCA figured quite prominently in my life. During the summer, mornings began there with swimming lessons and the smell of chlorine. Each Friday there was a test that was comprised of each student attempting to swim across the pool without stopping in order to advance to the next level. The first summer I attended, I could never pass but the second summer I finally did. During afternoons it was free swim and Mom would drop me off and also my two cousins when they were staying with us.

*   *   *

My cousins lived out of state. It was quite a different dynamic for me when they would stay with us for the summer. One was my age and the other a couple years older. We played with what we could find taking the chains of the swings off the swing set and lowering them to the ground pretending it was a spaceship or turning my room onto a submarine. As mentioned before, we sometimes also acted out movies I had made up. Each afternoon we got to pick something out of the candy drawer as a snack. Fourth of July was always a big deal and we lit bottle rockets watching them fly into the air and explode and then capped the day off by eating watermelon in the still quite warm evening.

My uncle, their father, was also a pastor. My Dad who was older took a much more fundamental approach to pastoring and my uncle was looser and more modern. He was also a visual artist and would design his own banners that he would hang in the nave of his church. He also played guitar in his services, something he eventually got my father to do on occasion. Dad really liked my cousins, one time when I was drawing, he came into my room and said that I should be more like them.

One summer we flip flopped and I was sent to Chicago instead of them coming here. I had to wear a button on my shirt indicating that I was a minor flying by myself. It was exhilarating being on the plane by myself and having the stewardesses keep an eye out for me. Once we landed and were taxiing to the gate, I could see my uncle and cousin waiting through the large window of the airport. We went to their house in one of the suburbs of Chicago where my older cousin and some friends were taking turns driving a go-kart. I was able to drive it myself although did not go near the speed that they were. I stayed in the room of the cousin my age on the second floor the parsonage located right next to the church building. We swam in an above ground pool of a friend of theirs which was a rarity for that city. We also went to a drive-in movie theater and they made popcorn at home that they brought with us in Tupperware. There was a pharmacy and store nearby we went into frequently and I brought my friend Laura back a souvenir that was a figure with a little sign that read 'I'm a lover not a fighter'. My older cousin played the piano. I had taken lessons a few years earlier and he taught me the treble-clef notes to "The Entertainer" and we would practice as a duet as he played the bass-clef. A couple times we spent the night in a tent in their backyard.

It was somewhat strange to be in a different state. The houses were noticeably older, the lawns were different not having the thick blades of grass and the shade of green I was accustomed to, and the people talked with an accent I had not heard before.

When it became August, it was almost time for me to go home. Those last few days were a heartache as it meant summer was ending, and seeing the cartoons that were shown on weekday afternoon television brought on such melancholy because it would soon be time to go back home and begin the school year.

*   *   *

In the car on the way to baseball practice that afternoon, I remembered the previous fall when my parents had signed me up to play tackle football also at the Y. During each practice, the coach had us all run from one side of the field to the other. One afternoon as we were finishing, I heard him laughing with the assistant coach and saying my name in a high-pitched voice while running in place with his hands up at his shoulders bouncing up and down. Apparently, this was how I looked when I ran. I didn't realize it and was completely embarrassed in front of the team and told myself to remember to never do that again. After the first couple of games, I began telling my Mom when I got home from school that I had a stomach-ache and couldn't go to practice. Eventually my parents let me stop playing, although we never actually talked about it. A few weeks later as I was going to Laura's school fall festival, I saw the coach across the street. When he saw me, he called over belligerently, "Did you just quit?" I replied, "Yeah" and nothing else bowing my head and just walking on.

But once I got to baseball practice today, thankfully it all went well and nothing bad happened. Mom picked me up and when we got home, we had dinner and again it was time for bed. As I was getting ready, I heard Mom and Dad arguing in the kitchen. I felt tired and was hoping I would fall asleep before I could think too much about things, but all I could do was toss and turn. Maybe Dad would stay up later tonight. I said a prayer that God would help me fall asleep, then waited and waited. I heard Dad straightening out the newspaper to read it. The television was on pretty low, but I could still hear a report about something called Watergate. I was hoping these sounds would help carry me to sleep. But then I heard the lamp being turned off and then nothing coming from the television. Dad had gone to his room. Now complete quiet.

Just me alone in the darkness. I squeezed my eyes shut and pulled the covers up to my neck. I didn't want to look out into my room, what if I saw a scary, menacing face looking back at me? Silence. Darkness. Feeling completely helpless. Many thoughts racing inside my head but none that would offer me refuge from the fear. And then what I wished I wasn't able to hear, the single word "Trey" that reverberated inside my head. Then came the dull thud from inside the closet and the clenching pain in my stomach and the gasping for air. I heard the sound of the faint creek as the closet door opened. Even though it was the last thing I wanted to do, I turned towards it. It was again difficult to see completely with such little light coming in, but I watched it lumber out. A blob of a head, torso, two arms and two legs. Then the rotting stench penetrating my room. It made its way to my desk. It picked up my markers and held them in its hand. It put them back down and picked up my schoolbook and ran its hand over it. It put that down and picked up some pictures that I had gotten back from being developed that were taken with my Brownie camera.

I tried to scream. Some kind of gasping sound came out. The Benji noticed, dropped the pictures and looked over at me. It hobbled towards the bed and all of a sudden jumped up on it. It stared down at me and I could feel malevolence coming off it in waves. Then it bent down and let out that guttural growl.

That's what did it and I scrambled between its legs feeling it's hands trying to catch me but not being able to. If it tried to pursue me, I didn't know as I ran down the hall and into my parent's room. I tried telling them as quickly as I could. I'm not even sure what I said. Then I fell to the floor. Dad was up and going to my room. All I could do was roll around. Then Dad was back and the light was on. Two hands picking me up and carrying me back to my bedroom. I jumped out of them and ran into the living room. I stood by the couch. Then both my parents were there.

"Trey this has to stop and you need to go to bed," Mom said

using that tone of hers that meant she has had quite enough.

"We don't care what you think you saw. There's nothing in your room." Dad's anger vibrated through each word he said. He was practically shaking with it and it felt like he was about to lose control of himself. It was the same sensation that I felt it coming off the Benji.

I began to cry. They were not going to help me. "You are breaking my heart," I sobbed.

"I've had enough of you," Dad said and they both walked away. Nothing but indifference from both of them about the pain I was in.

I sat down. I didn't sleep at all. I did not go back to my room until the morning when I heard Dad stirring in his room. My closet door was almost shut but not all the way.

6

Very little was said at breakfast. Mom didn't come in. Dad moved very stiffly. He had started giving me a half of cup of coffee in the mornings telling me to add milk and sugar to it, and though I really didn't like drinking it, I did and ate what was on my plate and then left for school.

In Ms. Barkley's class, we had started working on a play that we were going to perform in front of some of the other grades. It was about a trial and I played one of the lawyers for the defendant. I had one line that started with the phrase, 'may it please the court'. While we were rehearsing, I did my line and Miss Barkley started laughing and told me "you're jumping out of that chair so hard. Tone it back some."

I remember one time sitting on the bathroom counter looking into the mirror and practicing the voice and facial expressions of a character I had made up. Dad walked in with a strange look on his face and asked what I was doing. I told him I was going to be an actor when I grew up. He laughed at me. He stated that was way too difficult to do that and to put it out of my mind because I would never be able to make a living at it.

When I got home from school that afternoon, my parents told me that we were going over to their friend's house who had a daughter my age named Robin who I liked playing with quite a lot. We rang the front doorbell and Robin's dad let us in. He had black hair streaked with gray that was combed to the side and was always in such good humor. We walked past their dining room and I saw the yard rake leaning against the wall that I had seen Robin's mother use before on their green shag carpet. I also noticed that her parents would hold hands, something I never saw my parents do. While they visited in the living room, I heard

Dad talking about what beautiful young lady my sister was going to grow up to be, and Robin and I went to her room and decided to play sisters. We compared the mood rings that we had both recently gotten and then dressed up in outfits she had in her closet, pretending we lived together and arranging her room like it was our house. At some point her door opened and our parents were standing there looking in at us.

"What are you doing dressed like that?" my Dad loudly demanded. Robin's plastic tea set was out along with some of her dolls.

"We're just playing," I stammered.

"Get out of what you're wearing, now! That is not how a boy plays." He was making a production of it in front of them. I quickly went into the bathroom and changed. I went back to Robin's room where she was waiting for me.

Dad walked back in. "Don't you ever let me see you like that again."

It was uncomfortable in the car on the ride home. When Dad stopped at a light, he looked back at me. "I have an image I want my family to look like in front of my church. You aren't it, but I am going to make you it." He turned back around. Mom didn't say anything.

We got home and I went to my grandmother's room. She was sitting at her sewing machine. I sat down on the floor next to her. I rubbed my head where I had now started feeling the Benji.

She stopped her sewing. "What is bothering you?" she asked.

"I just feel so alone." I so wanted to tell her what was happening, but what if she said something to Dad? He would be so mad at me for talking to her about it.

"Well, you can always tell me. I may not be able to do much, but I can listen". She stopped talking and winced. "Sometimes what I have really hurts. When it does, I feel very alone too."

"There's this thing, this Benji, that comes out of my closet. I can feel it inside my head. I told Mom and Dad, but they don't believe me."

She sat back and thought for a moment, like she was sensing

something and deliberating about what to do. After a moment she said, "You need to protect yourself. If it is something that has gotten inside your mind, you must act immediately." She slowly moved her legs around so she was talking directly at me and winced again. "Close your eyes. See yourself in your mind's eye surrounded by white light. Say the words, 'my mind is safe and protected from all that would harm me'. Repeat those words throughout the day."

"What do I do when it comes out in my room?"

"You make it go back to where it came from."

"How do I do that?"

"You must show it your intention to send it back."

I thought about what she was saying for a moment. "You're the only person I've told this besides this kid from school."

"Only confide in who you absolutely trust. But I am also getting that you have always been afraid. That is not good. Fear begets fear."

I thought for a moment. "How do I not be afraid?"

"We all have something in our lives we must grapple with even if we don't want to. Something painful and personal. For me, it is this sickness. For you, it is what scares you. We must make it our goal to face it and get to the other side of it." She stopped for a moment. "This is what we do. We wake up and do this every day." She winced again but it was for a long time and she held on to the table her sewing machine was on.

"Thank you, Grandma, for believing me. I will do what you say." I gave her a hug and left because she looked very tired and I didn't want to stay any longer while she was not feeling good.

7

So I did the only thing I knew to do, and that was to just keep going.

I had joined the cub scouts a couple years ago and advanced to being a Webelo. We met once a week after school wearing our uniforms. At today's meeting, our den mother reminded us we were going to go on an overnight camping trip over the weekend. So on Saturday morning we met up in front of her house. Her husband was who would actually be taking us, and he had a large station wagon that all the boys fit in that pulled a trailer that contained our supplies. He brought along a teenage assistant who we had never met before.

We drove a couple of hours out of town and arrived at the camp site. We were each called on to help put up one of the two tents that we would stay in that night. Then we went and gathered firewood for the campfire later. It was a beautiful campground next to a lake. It was fairly cloudy the whole time and so never got too hot. After we found all the wood we would need, we went for a hike around the lake and for some reason I felt compelled to hold our camp leader's hand. I heard a couple of the boys laughing about me doing that as we completed the hike and headed back to camp.

He and his assistant made everyone dinner, and when we finished eating, we roasted marshmallows using wire hangers that were straightened out. The fire crackled and it felt nice to be outside next to it.

Our scout leader then stated it was time for the den to head up to take showers before going to sleep. I had never showered in a group before and stated I didn't want to do that. He said it would be fine, and we all headed up there. I had never taken my clothes off in front of anyone else and felt ashamed having to do so. Mom always said I was overweight and I worried what the other boys would say about me. Dad made me take my shirt off during the summer when he would chase me out of the house to go play outside, and I always tried as much as I could to not have the neighbors see me like that. There was a group shower and some of the boys stripped down and headed that way. But there were also a couple individual showers, so I took my towel, went into one of those and showered there.

I put my clothes back on and went to wait with the others in our troupe when two teenagers who looked like they were in high school came in. They got undressed and went into the group shower. As they did, I watched them, I had never seen an older boy's naked body before. I noticed the hair above their penises and then understood that is what was going to happened to me, and I didn't like that. But I also realized that looking at them made me feel good. They saw me watching them and began to laugh.

Our camp leader started to head out. I gathered my things and was one of the last to leave. We formed sort of a line making our way back to our campsite. One of the scouts that was behind me came and stood in front of me. I stopped walking.

"What a baby you are. Everybody got naked except you."

Another boy moved next to him. "I saw you looking at those two guys. That was weird. I know what you are." Although it was dark, I could hear the sneer in his voice. The other one grabbed my shirt.

"Do you know what we do with boys like you?" They started leading me toward the perimeter of the campsite where the forest started.

"If you make any noise, I will really hurt you, you can count on that."

When we got there, he pushed me to the ground. The other one kicked me in the leg. "Don't come back to camp. We don't want your kind around." Then he spit on me.

When they left, I got up. I wiped off my clothes the best I could and picked up my towel and soap. I didn't know what they meant when they said they knew what I was. What was my kind?

I started slowly walking back towards camp. I wondered what they would they do when they saw me. As I got closer, I did not see anyone so figured everyone had gone into their tent and went inside mine. I didn't see those two, thankfully they must be in the other one.

"What took you so long," one of the scouts asked me.

"I got sidetracked," was all I could think of to reply.

Our camp leader came in and announced it was lights out. He went back to his tent and his assistant stayed in ours. I got into my sleeping bag. I stayed awake listening to the crickets and finally at some point fell asleep.

When I awoke there was already activity outside. I went out and immediately scanned for the two boys from last night. They were sitting on a log and noticed me. They got a perverse grin on their faces, like they had put me in my place and thought it was funny. We had breakfast and then loaded everything up for the trip home.

Mom picked me up, and while we were still in the car our den mother came over. She had her small dog in her hand. She asked if I had a good time, and I lied and said I did.

8

The next Saturday I was getting ready to go the matinee like usual and heard my parents arguing again. Dad called my Mom stupid and slammed the door on his way out. On the way home from the theater, Mom and I stopped at one of Dad's parishioners, I don't remember why. It was in the same neighborhood where Laura lived. I noticed the houses were much nicer than ours. We sat down at her kitchen table and the two of them were talking when we saw her neighbor's kids outside. She started laughing because those kids had put dark makeup all over their bodies so it looked like they were Black. There weren't very many Black people in the area we lived in. I didn't understand why they would do something like that and why she thought it was funny.

When we got home, I asked Mom if Laura could come over. She said yes, so I called and asked and her Mom agreed. While I was waiting, I decided to write a letter to my friend who I had met when we were living in another state before this one. He had sent some pictures of him and his brothers, and in the background of one of them was a sign he drew of the radio station they listened to in their town. I thought about how Laura liked listening to the radio so much also. I wrote a letter back and sent a picture that I drew of their house. I addressed the envelope the way Mom taught me to using the word Master before my friend's name. I went and gave it to her to put in the mail. When Laura got here, she had a big brightly colored bag with her. When we went to my room, she started pulling out her two Barbies. We were just getting ready to play with them when all of a sudden Dad opened the door to my room. When he saw what we were doing, he raced over to me. I had one of the dolls in my hand.

"What did I tell you, I told you not to play with those!" he yelled. Then he slapped me across the face so hard that my glasses flew off. My face stung and I felt humiliated in front of Laura and started crying. "Put those away and dry up. Play with your own toys like I told you."

We put them back in the bag and I got out my markers and paper so we could draw pictures instead. Laura gave me a big hug and I could tell she felt very awkward about what had happened. I thought about asking her to stay for supper, but could tell that she wanted to go home.

The next day was Sunday and I got ready and put on my church clothes. We had our Sunday school class in one of the two back rooms in the parish hall. At the end we sang "They'll Know We Are Christians by Our Love". Our Sunday School teacher lived on a farm and brought one of her cows and a donkey once when us Sunday school kids performed our Christmas Eve program outside in the parking lot. When class was finished, I sat with Mom in the pew and watched as Dad led the church service and went to the pulpit to give the sermon which always seemed so long and repetitive. Sometimes he preached about what was going to happen on Judgement Day. I had once dreamt that it was Judgement Day. The sky was filled with ominous, dark clouds and God was actually Dad.

The next day when I was walking to get on my bike after school, I saw Jackie. He was crouched down tying his shoelace then stood up like he was about to run off.

"Hey Jackie," I called out.

"Can't talk," he said shrugging his shoulders, "Bruce is after me," then he sprinted away. I couldn't imagine why Bruce would want to fight Jackie of all people. I thought about that all the way home.

When I got there, Mom asked me to get her a loaf of bread from the grocery store. It was just a few blocks away, so I got back on my bike and drove there. As I was leaving the store, I put the bread in the basket and started to ride off, and then to my alarm I actually saw Bruce walking towards me. Before I could even try to turn around, he called out, "Hault!"

I stopped. He walked over to me.

"What are you doing here?"

"Getting bread for my Mom," I think I said.

He had his hands on the handlebars of my bike. Neither of us said anything.

Not knowing what else to do, I said, "Here you can have this," and put the change I had in his hand.

He looked at it and then back at me. "All right," he said and walked away.

I rode back home in shock by what just happened. Why did this have to happen with the one person I was so afraid of? I parked my bike in the garage and went to my room. I had some bubble gum I had also bought in my pocket and I threw it against the wall. I guess I looked upset when I came in the house because Dad came in my room.

"Did something happen when you were at the store" he asked with a puzzled look on his face.

The only thing I could think of was to tell him the truth. "This kid from school made me stop when I was trying to ride home. I gave him the change."

He paused. "Did he try and fight you?"

"No."

He looked at me with disappointment. "If some kid wants to fight you, you're just going to have to." He left.

The next day at school there was a presentation with another class where us students were to read aloud a poem that we had prepared. I had chosen a limerick about an old man who rides on a bear. I made a beard out of cotton puffs and brought one of my sister's teddy bears and pretended I was on its back when I performed the poem. The teachers actually ended up giving out three prizes, and I won best costume. The prize was that we were taken to the McDonald's next to the school for lunch. Two of the teachers bought us what we wanted. I was nervous and there were a few moments when I couldn't stop giggling. One of the other girls who had also won a prize gave me a stern look.

When I got home, I was going to tell Mom what happened

when she met me at the back door. "Grandma died today. She just didn't wake up this morning."

I went inside and sat down at the kitchen table. I looked at Mom trying to comprehend what she just said.

"Her body gave out. You'll need to come to the funeral."

I had never been to one before. How could she just die? I didn't understand.

"Your father is at the funeral home. We'll have dinner when he comes home."

I took my schoolbooks to my room and then went into hers. The bed was still unmade. There was a heaviness that penetrated the room, an air of permanence that she would not be coming back. I looked around stopping at her shelves and again took in what she had there. I noticed there were also some big books with gold lettering. I walked slowly down the hall back to my room and sat on the floor. I would never get to see or her again. I tried to remember all the things we had talked about since she moved in even before I told her about the Benji. As my eyes drifted around my room, I saw that small net with feathers at the very end of one of my shelves. She must have put it there, but I never noticed. I said out loud, "my mind is safe and protected from all that would harm me."

9

At the funeral, I had to wait at the back of the church with Mom to be ushered in once the service began. My cousins, aunts and uncles were there, and we sat in the front two rows. Dad led the service and I wondered if he was going to cry, but he never did. When we sung one of the hymns I began to, thinking of how often I could have gone into her room to see how she was feeling and ask if I could get her something, but I had never thought of doing that.

There was a potluck dinner in the parish hall afterwards. We sat at long tables like we always did. Both Laura and Robin were there with their families, and when we finished eating, they came over and hugged Mom and myself and shook Dad's hand. When it was over, Mom and I started walking back to the house with Mom holding my sister like we did after every church service. Dad always came home by himself later. I changed out of my suit and went back to the living room. Mom was sitting by herself just staring ahead which was strange because she always watched television when she was in here. My sister was in her room with her toys. I sat down on the couch but didn't say anything. We sat like that until Dad came home. He went and changed and came back out and sat down in his recliner. He told me to go and get him a beer from the refrigerator, which I did. It was completely quiet with all of us being in the house together. Dad seemed to be lost in thought.

"My sisters and brother are going back with their children in the morning," he said.

"It was so nice to see them," she answered.

I wondered if they would hold hands, but they didn't.

"We need to go through all of her things tomorrow."

After a moment I asked, "What did Grandma do before she

came to live with us?"

"She worked in a school cafeteria and after your grandpa died, she kept doing that. She moved in with my sister Lillian when her husband was killed. She then also helped my sister with her kids and around the house. That's when she got sick. That town is so small that she needed to come here for her treatment." I remembered we had taken a couple of trips there to visit. Grandma's room was in their converted garage. My aunt Lillian was a nurse and she had five children, my cousins. One was my age, and he was the one I played with the most although at times we all did in either their back or front yard. Their neighborhood always had a distinct scent from the trees that lined the street, but I never found out what kind they were.

"What was Grandpa like?" I asked. I had never got to meet him as he had died when I was a baby, and Dad never talked about what it was like being a kid in their family.

"He was a monster," he answered and turned on the television.

I wondered if we should talk more about Grandma, but Dad didn't seem like he wanted to. I thought about all the wonderful things Grandma cooked for us, the homemade bread and cookies. If my clothes got torn, she always sewed them up.

My parents sat there like that and I went to my room.

10

The next Saturday morning, Dad said we needed to go get new shoes for me. For the last few months, my feet began to really hurt at times, so much that it made me cry. Dad started having me soak my feet in Epson Salt and that helped for the moment, but a week later it would come back. Dad had sold shoes when he was younger and after examining me said that I had flat feet. We had to go across town to a shoe store that sold those type of shoes. We got there and I tried on some and Dad chose the ones he wanted. They were odd looking, very heavy and dark that would stand out from what the other kids were wearing. We drove home and I began thinking how awkward I was going to feel wearing them at school. When we were a block away from our house, I was looking out the window and saw Bruce going through the back door of one of the houses there. This meant he lived only a block away! The one person I dreaded most in the world lived this close to me. We pulled into the garage, I got out and went and sat on the swing set in the backyard. I guess I was there awhile because the sun began to set and I felt that foreboding feeling rise in my stomach. It would soon be night. I brought my little cars out and drove them all over the swing set as if it was some kind of giant racetrack. Dad was inside the garage at his work bench and came around to where I was, I guess to see what I was playing.

"Dad, it really embarrasses me when you punish me in front of other people. Would you please stop doing that in front of them?"

He didn't say anything, just looked at me and scowled. Then went back to what he was doing. It became time for dinner, after that I had some homework to finish and then it was time for bed.

Every day was like this now. I had never looked forward to going to school during the week, Saturdays were fine but then came Sunday and I was already not looking forward to going back. And now there was also this dreading of each day drawing to a close and the apprehension of the coming night.

I got in bed and tried to fall asleep, but like usual to no avail. It was the same night after night. Laying there and not knowing if I was going to fall asleep before Dad did, and then hearing him straighten things up, turn off the lamp and leave the living room. Then knowing I was completely alone in the darkness. Wondering if the Benji was going to come out. Having no one who would help me if it did.

And then tonight came that soft thud from inside the closet, the announcement of its arrival. Another sound as it tried to find the door handle and then the closet door slowly opening.

That putrid stench. Then it trudging out. It went to my desk. It picked up the bottle of seashells I had collected at the beach and ran its hands over it. It put that down. Then it picked up some pages I had drawn on. There was a fire in my chest and my throat was constricted at there not being anything I could do to stop this.

But then something new happened inside me. As I watched the Benji, I began to think about what my life had become. Of how much my father had shamed me in front of other people. How I was made fun of by other kids and how fearful Bruce made me feel. I thought about the words my grandmother had taught me. Then I felt a benevolent presence beside me, and I knew at once it was her. Her spirit was here giving me strength. Finally, someone was helping me. The paralyzing fear gave way.

"I don't want to be afraid anymore!"

I jumped out of bed and ran towards the Benji. I said as loudly as I could, "My mind is safe and protected from all that would harm me!" My arms were outstretched, and I ran into it, feeling that it was spongy like a corpse. I could see its eyes roll in disbelief as I started pushing it back into the closet. Its mouth lunged at me trying to bite, but I pulled back just enough. I kept repeating those words and pushing until it was all the way back in.

I don't know what happened after that. I came to as Dad was carrying me to the car. I heard my parents talking to me, but it was if they were very far away. They said I had blacked out. Then we were at the emergency room at the hospital, the same one where my sister was born. The doctor looked me over, it was as if everything was in slow motion. I heard him go over and tell my parents he couldn't tell exactly what was wrong with me, just that something must have upset me so much I fainted, and to take me home and watch over me. Mom made a pallet next to her on the floor of their bedroom. I stayed there that night and didn't go to school the next day, and slept there again the next night.

I don't remember much of the next few days. What happened had taken a lot out of me and it was taking some time for me to recover. The familiar rhythm returned of doing what needed to be done every day. I went back to school. I sang in music class and went to the front during math class to work out a problem on the chalk board. I came home and then Dad would also and we ate dinner and I finished homework and went to bed wondering if something bad was going to happen. Then one evening at dinnertime, Dad announced he had accepted a call to be the pastor at a church in Chicago and that we were going to move. We would be closer to those cousins. In only a few weeks a large 18 wheel moving truck pulled into our driveway. While the movers were inside the house, I walked up the metal ramp on the side of the truck and walked around inside. All of our belongings were going to go into this, and we were going to drive across the country. I spent one last night at Laura's house so we could say goodbye, and got together with Danny and we rode our bikes around the neighborhood one last time. Laura and I would keep in touch as we reached adulthood. I never saw Danny again.

The Benji never come back.

11

What is it that you remember when you think back on your childhood?

It's a little after midnight now. There's a glass in my hand, I swirl what's left of the alcohol in the melting ice and finish it off. It's not helping but it's there, always there. I'm in my apartment where I live alone.

Have been thinking about this all night long, what I just told you. The things we forget about our childhood until we really take the time to remember. You know, when we're starting out in our young adult lives, there's all this ambition as we start working at our jobs. There's not even an inkling inside that we might not be able to achieve all that we want to. That we won't receive all the desires of our hearts. It doesn't even begin to occur to us that we just might not have what it takes.

I guess it takes something really jarring to make us really go back to those forgotten memories. How early was it when you lost the innocence of being a child? So much so that you realize that the innocence was never really there.

I was so isolated being a pastor's kid. My parents didn't love me, I just wasn't what they wanted their first-born son to be. The expectations of a newly married couple in their early twenties back in the 1970's. It wasn't as if they weren't capable of it, as my sister grew up both Mom and Dad showered her with affection.

Did I say goodbye to Jackie before we moved? I don't remember if I did or even what his last name is. I didn't realize how much his friendship meant to me. How he helped me get through such a miserable childhood by just being himself. Now he's lost to me. Then there's what Laura and Robin meant to me by letting me play in the ways that let me be who I really was.

My father's attitude and actions towards me never changed as I grew older. Right after we moved to a small town during high school where I was having quite a bit of trouble fitting in, I was calling one of my friends in Chicago when he disdainfully told me, "make new friends." He was completely invested in my sister's life, but not mine. After a few surgeries as he got older, his health began to decline. After a second bout with a brain tumor, he needed assistance walking. It was so strange to see someone who was once such a force of nature be so weak. We never reconciled. On his death bed his wife called me, for he had divorced my Mom, and she stated that this was the time to tell him what I needed to. I told him that I loved him. The next day he died. I lived out of state and didn't go to the funeral.

I was a haunted boy. By my father's malice towards me. By being so different from other boys. By something that came out of my closet.

My child-self never thought about really checking in that closet to see how the Benji was getting in. Why didn't I check for some kind of hidden door, lift the carpet up? Maybe it came up from under the house.

But I did have a guardian spirit I didn't know was there.

Earlier this evening I pulled out the only drawing I had saved. It was one of the ones I had hung in my window, this one of Halloween. This was how I coped. By drawing and writing. It's how I expressed myself and it helped me get by.

So what comes after a childhood like that? I've never been able to form a lasting romantic relationship. The interest that somehow got piqued in him always fades away in a matter of weeks with the realization that I'm just a one trick pony. I've never able to become an actor because my father humiliated so much in front of other people that I can't get over the performance anxiety that was produced. I have not been able to feel in control of anything and that has provoked quite a bit of anxiety. I have no self-esteem. I'm barely successful at jobs which never seem to last.

There are two afternoons in my childhood that have stayed with me. One was in 1st grade when my class was playing across the street from the school in an empty lot. There was such a smell of honeysuckle in the air that day. I remember stopping in the middle of what I was doing and noticing that for a moment it felt like time was standing still. I realized that I was experiencing something important although I didn't know exactly what that was, just this sense of timelessness. It happened once again while I was playing in Laura's backyard one afternoon. Could it have been me going through these memories of my childhood so intently that I could feel it back while it was actually happening? I remember having read somewhere that time isn't really linear, that it's all happening at once and that it is more accurate to imagine time as thread spools, like from my grandmother's sewing machine, stacked up in a vertical column. If everything is happening at one time, and if I send love to myself as a little boy, perhaps I could actually feel it then? Maybe it's silly to think this way. Maybe it's not.

There's another result of my childhood and that is I'm a bit obsessive-compulsive. Everything has its proper place in my apartment. I know exactly where everything sits on my desk. And here's the thing...some have moved a bit. A picture frame, a coaster. Not put back exactly where they go.

I'm sitting on my couch looking at the closet and wondering if I was the one who left it open slightly.

What happens to us as children never really goes away. Does it?

12

I thought I was finished with this, but now it's back. As if my days aren't hard enough to get through, now I'm back to dreading what could happen at night. Trying desperately to fall asleep, and when I do, it's fitful at best. And what is it that's underneath this? Rage. I am seething that what I suffered with so much as a child has returned. I thought I paid my dues. Here I am a grown man, but my life hasn't changed from when I was a child. It's the exact same thing.

Sometimes it's actually funny that I still can't get over this. It stops being funny when I'm in bed closing my eyes and every time I'm about to fall asleep, my body jerks and I open my eyes and look around for what might be coming for me out of the closet. Then laying there and knowing that whatever time I finally do fall sleep, it won't be enough to keep me from being exhausted the next day.

Of course I have now checked the closet. I found nothing. My apartment is on the ground floor. Is there another way in?

I go through the day in a daze. I shudder at night. Maybe this is how it ends, by me going mad. Howling at the atrocities I've endured all my life. No one hearing me or caring. Who's going to save me now? I haven't felt my grandmother's presence since that night. I haven't felt much of anything.

It is morning and I go to my job at the insurance company. I'm always just a few minutes ahead of when I need to be there. I turn on the computer in my bland cubicle and take a sip of the coffee that's already getting cold. My eyes shut. Then I hear my name coming from my manager standing right beside me. It startles me and I do my best to look like I'm unaffected and he tells me he needs to talk to me in his office. I follow him and look at the back of his shirt already wrinkled for this early in the morning. I sit in the chair on the other side of his desk and notice his boss sitting at the back of the room with a large folder in his hands and then look back to him as he starts talking about numbers and who's joined the company most recently and how this is never easy and they all wish me the best and security will accompany me as I clean out my desk and leave the building. I don't feel anything. The guard and I walk out of his office and he hands me a box. There's not much to gather up. The coffee in the paper cup still sits there from when I was an employee. A few eyes glance up at me from people I never really got to know. It was nothing personal, I just didn't have it in me to want to get that involved with them. We take the elevator down. It wasn't a bad job; I've had much worse. I could have stayed with it a few years.

My car is not too far away in the parking garage. I get in and put the box in the back seat. I think about how much money I have in the bank. I check on my phone, not a lot, but there's some. I'll file for unemployment. I drive home. I put the stuff away and I sit on the couch and look at the closet. I pull out a credit card and call the phone number to check the balance. It's about what I thought and it gives me a little more cushion. I get back on my phone and amazingly find a flight for later in the afternoon. I also book a night at the cheapest hotel I can find. I get up and throw some clothes inside my small suitcase.

It's not very far to the airport so I take a ride share. When we arrive, I get out and once through the screening line I get to my gate. I have a few hours to wait so I sit down. But then it's time to board. My boarding pass gets scanned and through the jet bridge I go and onto the plane. Once I put my suitcase away and get settled in my seat, we start to move and are soon in the air. I stare forward the entire time. We land, I grab my bag and walk out and go straight to the car rental counter. Once I get in the car, it's to the hotel where I check in, unload what's in the suitcase, and then get back into the car.

The facility is about a thirty-minute drive away. The small town where it's located is full of some of the prettiest trees I've ever seen, today swaying in the sunny afternoon breeze. I park, go in through the front door and check with the nurse's station. I am told she is in her room. I walk down the hall, her room is almost to the end and on the left. She is sitting in her wheelchair. She has her sweater on. The television is on but turned down very low. I pull over a chair and sit directly in front of her.

At first she doesn't even register there is anyone there, but finally she blinks and does. She hasn't remembered me now for about three years. There is no flicker of recognition in her eyes, just a mild response of the presence that's in front of her. Her graying hair is longer than I remember, her shoulders a bit more hunched over.

"Hello Mom, it's Trey."

She mumbles something unintelligible. I take her hands in mine, her skin is cool. We sit like this for a few moments. There is not much sound coming from the hallway. It doesn't matter if I say anything, she won't understand. She is locked in a world unto herself. I wonder if she feels lonely. My sister has said she comes here once a week to check on Mom, but apart from that there is no one else that does. I put her hands back in her lap.

For an hour or so we stay like this. Then I tell her goodbye. I tell her it is all right whenever she is ready to go. I think about what my grandmother would want me to do, so I imagine Mom's mother and father around her with other relatives that she loved. I ask them to help keep safe and to help her cross over when it's time. I tell her that I love her, just as I told my father as he was dying. Because somehow despite what happened in my childhood and although she never tried to protect me from my father, I do. I put the chair back and stand in the doorway and look at her.

I get back into the rental car. It takes a little less than an hour to get to the house. The sun is starting to set now, but there will still be enough light. I park on the side of the street a half a block down and slowly walk towards it. There is a chain link fence completely around it now and bricks that cover the exterior. My old room sits stoically facing the street, but there are now blinds on the window which are closed. It will not allow me to peek inside as if telling me my time here is done. The church was bought by some company and there is a metal warehouse in the middle of what used to be the empty field.

I stand there until it gets completely dark. Then I also say goodbye to this house and what happened here.

Back at the hotel I lay in bed and again feel that presence at the front of my head that I thought had gone away.

Morning rush hour traffic is much worse than I remembered, but I make it on time and board the flight back home. Again, I just stare forward and before I know it, we are landing. Once at home, I unpack and put the suitcase away under the bed. It's barely early afternoon. But I sit on the couch and face the closet.

There is no fear now. I expect there won't be either once the night comes. What's there now is an emptiness. A void where all the years of a life well lived should be. Not this nothingness of a man who is lost and in his late fifties. I have no idea what will happen during Act III of my life. Will I too become a victim of a brain tumor that took my father? Or of the Alzheimer's that has taken over my mother? Will I be able to find a man who I can love? There's no way to know. But I do know this. When the Benji comes out, I will get up, run to it and push it back in again. I will say my grandmother's words. Then for the first time as an adult, I feel her presence again.

We are truly never alone, and I choose to write an ending for myself that no matter what does happen, I am happy.